Golden Egg Hunt

by R. P. Anderson
illustrated by Gayle Middleton

HarperFestival®
A Division of HarperCollinsPublishers

It was springtime in Ponyville,
and the ponies were excited.
Today was the Golden Egg Hunt!

Cherry Blossom hoped she would be
the lucky pony to find the Golden Egg this year.
She passed a cherry tree in full bloom. "Maybe that
means good luck for me," she said, giggling to herself.

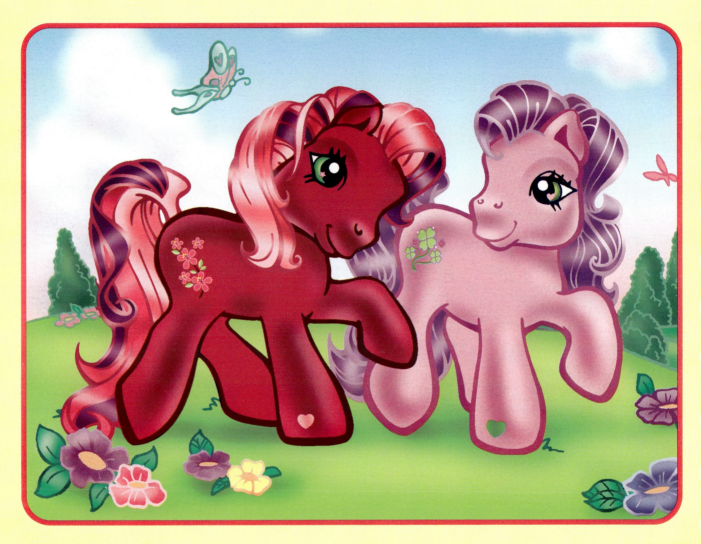

Cherry Blossom was almost to Celebration Castle when she met a friend. "Serendipity, I wish I were as lucky as you. You've found the Golden Egg three years in a row. How do you do it?"

"I look high and I look low. And I look round and round!
And when I think I've looked everywhere I can,
then I look some more."
"Thanks, Serendipity! Maybe I'll be as lucky as you,"
said Cherry Blossom.

Celebration Castle looked beautiful!
Meadowbrook was picking flowers with Wysteria.
Pinkie Pie was hanging streamers from the windows.

Sunny Daze and Twinkle Twirl were
organizing baskets under a cherry tree.

Inside, the kitchen was full of activity.
There were eggs everywhere!
Eggs in every pattern and color were piled high,
with the Golden Egg on top!

"We're almost done," said Cupcake.
"This will be the best Golden Egg Hunt ever!"
cheered Sweetberry.

Cherry Blossom watched excitedly
as the eggs were gathered for hiding.

Maybe this year she would be
as lucky as Serendipity and find lots of eggs!

Cupcake, Sweetberry, and Strawberry Swirl
hid the eggs carefully outside.

Inside, the rest of the ponies were waiting expectantly.
Who would win the hunt this year?

At last the eggs were all hidden!
"It's time to start the Golden Egg Hunt!"
shouted Strawberry Swirl.
"On your mark, get set, go!"

The ponies ran in every direction.
Uh-oh! Poor Cherry Blossom!
Everywhere she turned, a pony was running by her.

"I found a green one!" Minty squealed.
"I found a polka-dot one!" Sunny Daze cried.

"There are so many to find!" they both said.
And off they went.

Just then, Cherry Blossom spotted a great place to look.
Minty and Sunny Daze had rushed past it!

But as she got closer, Sparkleworks burst from
the bush carrying the eggs she had just found.
"Hi, Cherry Blossom," she called.

Suddenly, Serendipity dashed around the corner, ran right into Cherry Blossom, and dropped all her colorful eggs. "I'm sorry, Cherry Blossom. I didn't see you there. Oh dear, which eggs are yours and which ones are mine?"

Cherry Blossom was sad.
"They're all yours. I've looked high and low and round and round and haven't any found eggs at all. I'm just not as lucky as you, Serendipity."

Serendipity had an idea. "What if we look together? When you look high, I'll look low. When you look round one way, I'll look round the other way. I'm sure between the two of us we'll find the Golden Egg in no time!"

"I have an idea!" said Cherry Blossom . The ponies raced
to the corner of the garden. And there, resting in the
cherry tree, was the Golden Egg!
Cherry Blossom found it!

"You see, Cherry—you're a lucky pony, too,"
said Serendipity. Cherry Blossom smiled.
"Lucky to have a good friend like you!" she said.